Animated Classics

DISNEY

Tim Burton's The Nightmare Before Christmas

studio
INTERNATIONAL

Studio Fun International
An imprint of Printers Row Publishing Group
A division of Readerlink Distribution Services, LLC
9717 Pacific Heights Blvd, San Diego, CA 92121
www.studiofun.com

Printers Row Publishing Group is a division of Readerlink Distribution Services, LLC.
Studio Fun International is a registered trademark of Readerlink Distribution Services, LLC.

All notations of errors or omissions should be addressed to Studio Fun International,
Editorial Department, at the above address.
Special thanks to Tim Burton and the Walt Disney Animation Research Library staff for
providing the artwork for this book.

ISBN: 978-0-7944-4825-7
Manufactured, printed, and assembled in Dongguan, China.
First printing, June 2021. RRD/06/21
25 24 23 22 21   1 2 3 4 5

This book belongs to

_____

The Art of Tim Burton's The Nightmare Before Christmas

Following the completion of the short film *Vincent* in 1982, Tim Burton, who was employed at Walt Disney Feature Animation, wrote a three-page poem titled "The Nightmare Before Christmas." Working with production designer Rick Heinrichs, Burton created concept art, storyboards, and character models for the poem, which he shared with Disney animator Henry Selick. Burton left the studio in 1984, but he often thought about the project. In 1990, Burton and Selick teamed up to create Skellington Productions and produce the story as a full-length, stop-motion film, with Selick directing. Joe Ranft was brought on as storyboard supervisor with Eric Leighton supervising the animation. Burton and Selick wanted the production design to resemble a pop-up book, with inspiration being drawn from sources including German Expressionism and Dr. Seuss. Production began in 1991, with twenty soundstages used for filming. A total of 109,440 frames were taken for the film, using 227 puppets. Jack Skellington had around 400 heads, allowing the puppet to express every possible emotion. Since its initial release, Tim Burton's *The Nightmare Before Christmas* has gone on to receive critical acclaim, with audiences praising the creativity of its visual storytelling and innovative use of stop-motion animation. Throughout this book you can see the concept art, story sketches, and puppets from Skellington Productions artists.

Animated Classics

Disney

Tim Burton's The Nightmare Before Christmas

studio fun
INTERNATIONAL

In a land very, very far away, there is a terrifying place called Halloween Town.

Every year the ghoulish creatures who live there work tirelessly to make Halloween, the most important day of every year, a spooky surprise.

After one successful Halloween night, their leader, Jack Skellington, rode into town with his fearsome pumpkin costume ablaze. Ghouls, goblins, werewolves, and witches were gathered in the town square to celebrate this year's night of fright. The admiring crowd of monsters cheered as Jack leaped from his wooden horse and doused the flames in a fountain.

"Great Halloween, everybody," said the Mayor, who had two faces.

"I believe it was our most horrible yet," added Jack Skellington.

"Thanks to you, Jack!" replied the Mayor.

·WITCH·

Everyone in Halloween Town thought Jack Skellington was a frightening pumpkin king. They crowded around him to express how much they adored him. But Jack had heard it all before.

From the edge of the crowd, a rag doll named Sally watched Jack, her heart filled with longing.

She admired Jack from a distance.

Suddenly, Dr. Finkelstein, an evil scientist, grabbed hold of Sally's arm. "The deadly nightshade you slipped me wore off, Sally," he said.

Dr. Finkelstein had created Sally in his laboratory. In return, he expected Sally to be his loyal companion—forever. She tried to escape his grasp, but Dr. Finkelstein refused to let go. He started to pull Sally away from the crowd.

Thinking quickly, Sally pulled out the threads that attached her rag doll arm to her body. Eventually her arm detached, allowing her to run from Dr. Finkelstein. She fled to the graveyard while the arm she left behind knocked Dr. Finkelstein on the head several times.

In the square, Jack was still surrounded by the crowd as they continued to shower him with praise. But none of the compliments and good cheer mattered to Jack. Like Sally, he wanted to escape.

While the Mayor made an announcement, Jack took the opportunity to slip away.

"Nice work, bone daddy," a decomposing musician called after him.

"Yeah, I guess so. Just like last year," Jack replied.

Jack walked forlornly through the creaky metal gate of the graveyard. He followed the path to a tomb that looked like a doghouse. With a pat on his leg, Jack summoned Zero from his tomb. Zero was Jack's ghost dog, who had a glowing orange pumpkin nose and long, floppy ears.

As Jack walked, he boasted to Zero of his fame throughout the world as the king of fear. But Jack was bored of making people scream all the time. He wanted more than being the Pumpkin King. He wanted something different.

Jack felt an important piece was missing from his life. Even though he was the most famous frightener in all the world, it wasn't enough. A feeling of emptiness continued to haunt him. He thought no one in Halloween Town could possibly understand.

But someone did understand.

Sally had heard everything from behind a gravestone. She knew exactly how Jack felt. But Sally was too timid to reveal herself, so she silently watched as Jack walked into the forest of skeletal trees with Zero floating behind him.

***

"Sally!" Dr. Finkelstein called when he heard her return to his castle. "You've come back."

"I had to," Sally said, yearning to be reunited with her limb.

He led her to his laboratory, where he reattached her arm.

When Sally told Dr. Finkelstein that she was feeling restless, he dismissed it.

"It's a phase, my dear. It'll pass," Dr. Finkelstein said. "We need to be patient, that's all."

But Sally didn't want to be patient.

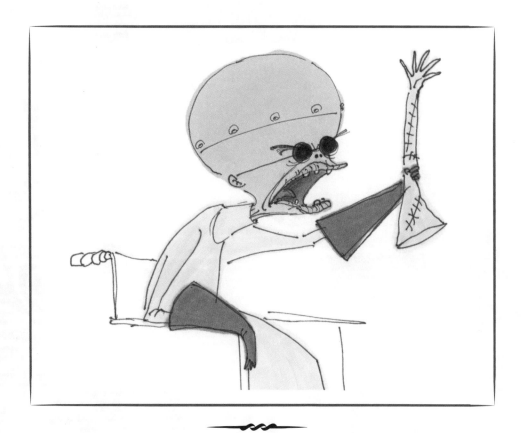

Early the next morning, the Mayor arrived at Jack's house to discuss the plans for next Halloween. After all, there were only 364 days to get everything in order. He climbed up the steps and rang the bell, but there was no answer. The Mayor, starting to get frustrated, pounded on the door. Still, there was no answer.

The Mayor did not realize it, but Jack was not home. In fact, Jack hadn't been home all night.

At the very edge of Halloween Town, the pumpkin sun blazed above the skeletal trees of the forest. Jack yawned, tired after a long night of wandering.

Suddenly, he found himself in a place unlike any he had been before.

"What is this?" Jack wondered as he stepped into a clearing. All around him stood trees with strange, colorful pictures carved into their trunks.

One was carved with a pretty egg. Another one was carved with a plump turkey. But one carving stood out to Jack more than any other. It was a brightly decorated green tree with a yellow star on top.

As Jack looked closer, he saw that the carvings were in fact doors with shining doorknobs.

Curious, Jack took hold of the doorknob on the tree door, turned it, and pulled. When it opened, Jack leaned inside to see where it led.

But all he could see was total darkness. Jack stepped back, disappointed. Then a flurry of snowflakes swirled out from the tree, circled around his body, and pulled him inside. The door slammed shut behind him, leaving Zero in the forest alone.

Down Jack tumbled as spiraling snowflakes eddied around him.

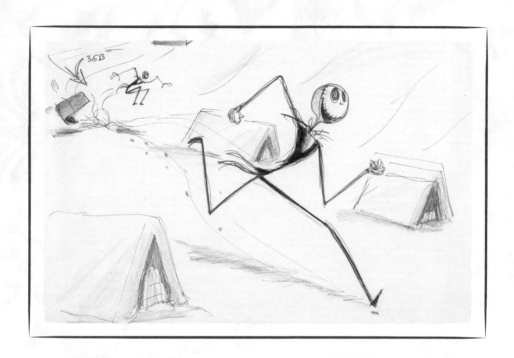

Jack landed with a thump. A bright flash blinded him for a moment. As his sight returned, he found himself sitting on top of a hill covered in a strange, white, powdery substance. Then he looked out over the most cheerful town he had ever seen. Colorful lights lit up all the buildings while smiling creatures glided around a tree decorated with all sorts of shiny objects. He grabbed a handful of the white powder and took a bite. It was delightful!

Jack stood for a better view and then lost his balance. He slid down the hill toward the town.

As he examined the town further, Jack wondered if he was dreaming. All around him, people were laughing and singing. It was nothing like dark and gloomy Halloween Town. Everything was bright and cheery. There were no monsters, no witches, and nobody was scared.

Jack wanted to know more about this mysterious place he had accidentally discovered. But where was he?

Not looking where he was going, Jack crashed into a red-and-white-striped signpost.

" 'Christmas Town'?" Jack read.

Then a nearby door opened, and laughter filled the air. But this wasn't a piercing witch's cackle like Jack was used to. This laugh was . . . jolly.

Back in Halloween Town, the search was on for the missing Pumpkin King, led by the Mayor.

"We've got to find Jack," the Mayor declared to his citizens. "Is there anywhere we've forgotten to check?"

They had already checked every mausoleum, the sarcophagi, and the pumpkin patch. A vampire even peeked behind the cyclops's eye, but Jack wasn't there. He seemed to have completely vanished.

"It's time to sound the alarms!" cried the Mayor. With that, the alarm let out a screeching noise that carried throughout the town.

High in Dr. Finkelstein's castle, Sally heard the alarm.

Longing for her share of the excitement, she slipped deadly nightshade into her master's soup once again.

Sally presented the soup as she entered Dr. Finkelstein's lab. But something about the smell of the soup made the scientist suspicious.

"Until you taste it, I won't swallow a spoonful," he said, holding out a spoonful of soup to her.

Sally reached for the spoon but knocked it to the ground. When she bent down to pick it up, she pulled a spoon filled with holes from her sock. She dipped it into the bowl. Then Sally took a big, fake sip.

"See? Scrumptious," she said, placing the bowl in front of him. Sally watched with delight as Dr. Finkelstein gulped it down. Soon he would be asleep.

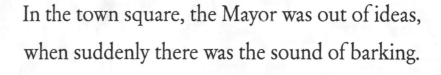

In the town square, the Mayor was out of ideas, when suddenly there was the sound of barking.

It was Zero!

Zero flew into Halloween Town with Jack following close behind, riding a snowmobile.

The Mayor demanded to know where Jack had been as a crowd gathered around them.

"Call a town meeting, and I'll tell everyone all about it," Jack said.

There was no time to waste. The Mayor immediately drove through the town to tell everyone about the meeting.

Dr. Finkelstein slept soundly as Sally sneaked out to join the meeting. Soon the whole town was gathered, eagerly awaiting Jack's big announcement.

"Listen, everyone," Jack said as he strode onto the stage. "I want to tell you about Christmas Town."

He began to explain the sights and the sounds and the warmth he had felt when he was there.

Everyone gasped at the present and the stocking Jack showed them. They wondered what horrible things they could put inside.

Jack told them that Christmas was nice and not frightening. But the citizens of Halloween Town didn't understand.

Unsure how to explain, Jack told them about the leader of Christmas Town. Jack had not met this ruler, but his vivid description was terrifying. He said the people of Christmas Town called their king "Sandy Claws."

The crowd was delighted. But Jack knew they were still missing something.

Later, in front of a fire, Jack searched through his books for a better way to explain Christmas. He wondered if science might help.

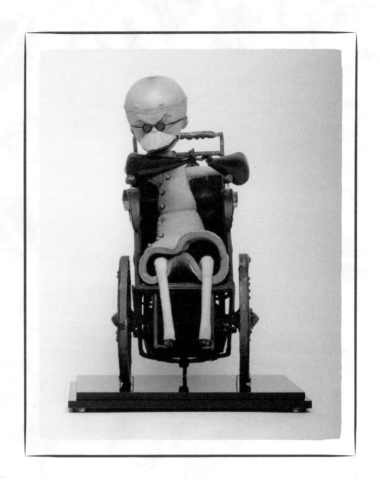

The next morning, Dr. Finkelstein locked Sally in a dungeon to make sure she never poisoned him again. As he secured the lock, his doorbell rang.

It was Jack. He wanted to conduct a series of experiments and needed to borrow some equipment. The evil scientist gave Jack everything he needed while Sally listened.

At home, Jack crushed holly berries under a microscope, sliced open a teddy bear, and boiled an ornament over a Bunsen burner. He made all kinds of observations, but he didn't know what any of it meant.

From her dungeon, Sally saw the glowing light from Jack's experiments. She decided to make him some provisions.

Through the window of her cell, Sally lowered the basket of food to the ground and leaped after it. When she landed on the cobblestones with a soft thud, her rag doll limbs separated from her body. But all was not lost. Sally picked up her pieces and sewed herself back together.

Sally took her basket to the Pumpkin King's window. Jack brought it inside, but when he looked out to thank Sally, she was gone.

Hidden behind a wall, Sally began pulling the petals off a dead flower. She wondered if she would ever have the courage to tell Jack how she felt.

Suddenly, the flower she held turned into a Christmas tree. Then it burst into flames. All that remained was a charred stick. She stared at it, worried what the vision might mean.

Meanwhile, Jack had not left his house in days. The people of Halloween Town worried about their pumpkin king.

In his makeshift lab, Jack felt frustrated. He was no closer to discovering the meaning of Christmas. Eventually, Jack decided that it didn't matter whether or not he understood the magic of Christmas, as long as he believed in it.

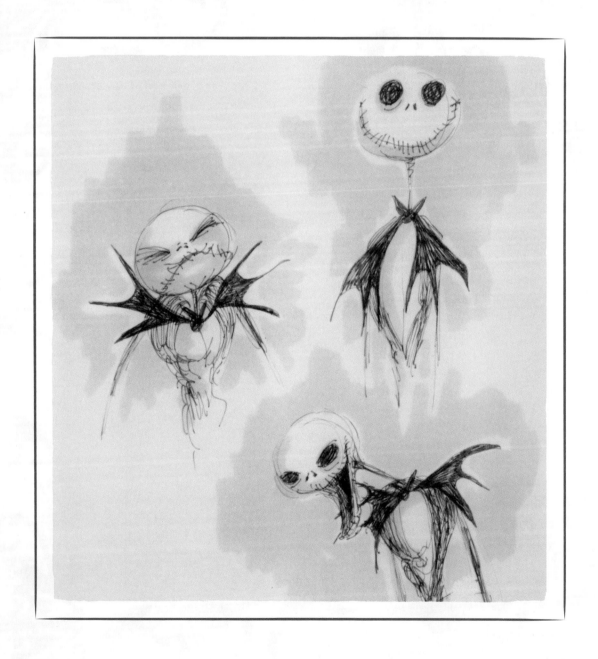

He believed in Christmas so much that he was sure he could improve it. Jack knew what he had to do.

He threw open the window and announced, "Eureka! This year, Christmas will be ours!"

There was a lot to be done, and Jack had jobs for everyone. The whole town lined up to receive their tasks.

Jack asked the vampires to make dolls and Dr. Finkelstein to make the reindeer.

"How horrible our Christmas will be!" cheered the Mayor.

"No, how jolly!" said Jack, correcting him.

Jack assigned his most important task to Halloween

Town's best trick-or-treaters, Lock, Shock, and Barrel. Jack wanted them to kidnap Sandy Claws.

Jack made them promise to tell no one about their mission, especially their master, Oogie Boogie. Then Jack sent them on their way.

But the trio had tricked Jack. They had crossed their fingers behind their backs as they'd made their promise. It was a promise they had no intention of keeping.

Meanwhile, Jack had a task for Sally. He wanted her to sew him his very own Sandy Claws costume.

Sally told Jack the details of her terrible vision. "It's going to be a disaster," she warned.

But Jack was too excited to listen. "I have every confidence in you," he said.

"But it seems wrong to me, very wrong," Sally said as she walked away.

Jack continued to hand out tasks to the townspeople when Lock, Shock, and Barrel returned with a walking bathtub carrying a mysterious sack. But when they opened it, there was no Sandy Claws. Instead, out hopped a pink bunny carrying a basket of eggs. The bunny, terrified at his surroundings, hopped right back into the bag.

"Take him back!" Jack commanded. He apologized to the shaking bunny inside the sack and sent them on their way.

***

As the big day drew closer, the two worlds—Halloween Town and Christmas Town—worked hard to create their versions of Christmas. But while the toys built in Christmas Town were guaranteed to bring delight, the citizens of Halloween Town made gifts that would cause terror. Halloween Town was making Christmas the only way it knew how—with possessed toys. It was making Christmas scary.

On Christmas Eve, final preparations were being made. Ghosts and mummies rushed to the town square with their ghoulish gifts to place in Jack's sleigh. Unlike the jolly red sleigh in Christmas Town, Jack's sleigh was black and built from a coffin pulled by reindeer skeletons.

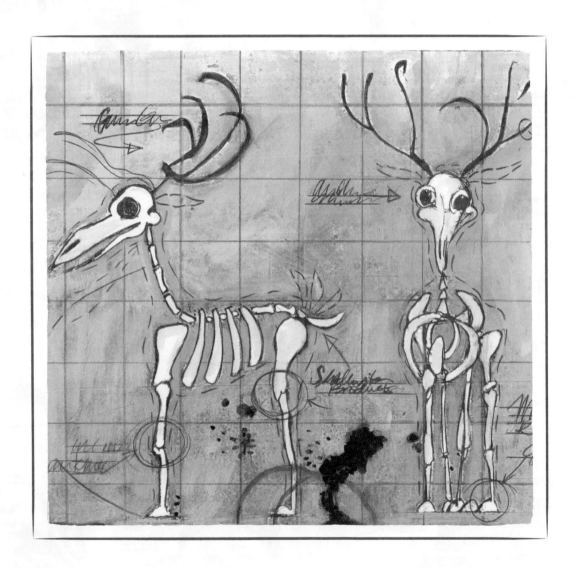

Christmas Town was almost ready too. Santa was checking his nice-and-naughty list when his doorbell rang.

"Now who could that be?" wondered Santa as he got up from his chair.

"Trick or treat!" cried Lock, Shock, and Barrel on Santa's doorstep. The treacherous trick-or-treaters bundled Santa into a sack, threw him into their walking bathtub, and raced back to Halloween Town.

✳✳✳

Meanwhile, Sally put the finishing touches on Jack's Sandy Claws costume.

"You don't look like yourself, Jack. Not at all," she said.

"Isn't that wonderful?" cried Jack.

"Jack, I know you think something's missing, but . . . ," Sally began.

"You're right. Something is missing. But what?" asked Jack, studying his reflection.

Then he heard a cry.

"Jack! Jack! This time we bagged him!" Lock, Shock, and Barrel had returned from Christmas Town.

"Let me out!" demanded Santa Claus as he burst out of the sack.

Jack immediately approached Santa. He couldn't believe he was finally meeting him! "Why, you have hands. You don't have claws at all!" exclaimed Jack as he shook Santa's hand.

Santa was very confused. He had no idea where he was.

"You don't need to have another worry about Christmas this year. Consider this a vacation, Sandy, a reward. It's your turn to take it easy," Jack explained.

"But there must be some mistake!" said Santa.

Lock, Shock, and Barrel started to pack Santa up again.

Just then, Jack noticed what he had been missing. He whisked Santa's hat from his head. Then he sent him on his way.

"This is worse than I thought. Much worse," said Sally, watching as Lock, Shock, and Barrel carried Santa away. Then she got an idea.

At their tree house, Lock, Shock, and Barrel tried to get Santa into the chute leading to Oogie Boogie's lair.

"I think he might be too big!" Shock said.

"No, he's not. If he can go down a chimney, he can fit down here!" Lock said, thumping Santa with a plunger.

With a mighty shove, the trick-or-treaters squashed Santa into the pipe. He landed with a thud on Oogie Boogie's roulette wheel.

Oogie was a mean creature so terrible that all of the ghosts, goblins, witches, and werewolves were frightened of him. His body was a shapeless sack, bursting at the seams with nasty insects, and his gaping mouth had a slithering snake for a tongue.

Oogie immediately started teasing Santa. With no way to escape, Santa begged Oogie to think of the children who were relying on him to deliver their gifts for Christmas morning, but Oogie refused to let him go.

Above, in the town square, people couldn't wait for Christmas to begin. Everyone, that is, except Sally.

While nobody was looking, Sally crept toward the fountain and emptied a bottle labeled "Fog Juice" into the water. A thick cloud of fog began to pour out of the fountain.

Sally slipped back into the crowd as Jack emerged from his coffin sleigh.

"Think of us as you soar triumphantly through the sky," began the Mayor, wishing Jack farewell. But the Mayor was unable to finish his speech. The fog from the fountain had descended on the town. It was so thick that he couldn't read the page in his hand.

Jack was distraught. They couldn't take off under these conditions. The reindeer wouldn't be able to see an inch in front of their noses. The crowd groaned while Sally let out a sigh of relief.

Zero rushed to Jack's side as he lamented his ruined plans. Jack tried to shoo the dog away, but then he noticed a light shining through the fog.

"My, what a brilliant nose you have," Jack said, looking at Zero's glowing snout. "The better to light my way." Jack sent Zero to the head of his skeleton reindeer team and, before Sally could stop him, soared into the sky.

Sally was convinced something tragic was going to happen to Jack, and that she and Jack would never find a way to be together.

High above a town in the normal world, Jack flew into the night, racing through the clouds. He brought his sleigh down on a snow-covered rooftop with a loud thump. It was time to deliver his first present. He hoisted his sack of presents onto his back and hopped down the chimney with ease.

A boy watched as Jack placed presents around the room. Jack spotted the boy and handed him a present tied with a black bow before disappearing up the chimney.

"And what did Santa bring you, honey?" the boy's mother asked.

The boy reached into the box and pulled out a shrunken head. His parents shrieked in terror.

Jack flew from house to house, leaving shocking gifts and terrified screams in his wake.

Calls soon flooded the police station as news of the skeleton Santa imposter spread. The authorities advised people to lock their doors to keep Jack out.

From the surface of an enchanted cauldron, the citizens of Halloween Town watched as Jack traveled from chimney to chimney, leaving fear instead of laughter in his wake.

Then they heard an announcement from a news presenter, "Reports are pouring in from all over the globe that an imposter is shamelessly impersonating Santa Claus, mocking and mangling this joyous holiday."

Jack's friends cheered. But Sally did not cheer.

Instead, she listened in horror as the news presenter continued, "Police assure us that, at this moment, military units are mobilizing to stop the perpetrator of this heinous crime."

Someone needed to help Jack. Sally got an idea. She needed to find Sandy Claws.

Jack flew on as searchlights swept the sky. Then the bright flashes and loud booms of exploding missiles filled the air.

"They're celebrating! They're thanking us for doing such a good job!" Jack cried, swerving to avoid a missile. "Whoa! Careful down there. You almost hit us," Jack called.

Beneath Halloween Town, Santa Claus hung from a hook in Oogie Boogie's lair while the monster played a cruel dice game with his fate. Oogie was about to roll the dice when he heard a noise behind him.

"My, my! What have we here?" Oogie ogled when he saw a shapely leg poking into his lair.

While Oogie was distracted, a pair of hands slid down the rope to untie Santa.

It was Sally. "I'll get you out of here," she whispered.

Oogie tickled the foot, but the leg came away in his hand. Oogie turned to see Santa climbing a ladder with Sally. He was about to escape!

Consumed with rage, Oogie took a breath so deep it sucked Santa and Sally back into his lair.

***

High above the normal world, Jack continued to swerve to avoid the missiles.

He quickly realized they were aiming for him! Suddenly, a direct hit blew his sled to pieces.

In Halloween Town, Jack's friends watched as Jack fell from the sky.

"Terrible news, folks! The worst tragedy of our times," announced the Mayor as he drove throughout the town. "Jack has been blown to smithereens!"

In the normal world, the police announced their own terrible news—there was no sign of the real Santa Claus. Christmas would have to be canceled.

***

Jack awoke, surrounded by the burned remains of his sleigh. He wondered how he could have been so wrong. He had tried to be something he wasn't and had failed.

Jack decided to go back to doing what he did best, being the Pumpkin King. But first he raced back to Halloween Town through the doors of a grave. He needed to set things right. After all, Christmas wasn't over yet.

News of Jack's demise drifted down to Oogie's lair, where the monster had tied Santa and Sally next to a pit of lava. Oogie rolled the dice, hoping for a high number, which would send the pair into the lava according to his rules.

When a low number appeared, Oogie slammed his fist on the table and the dice bounced to show the number he wanted. The game was rigged.

"Looks like I won the jackpot!" Oogie laughed. "Bye-bye, dollface and sandman." He pulled a lever to send Santa and Sally into the lava pit. When he didn't

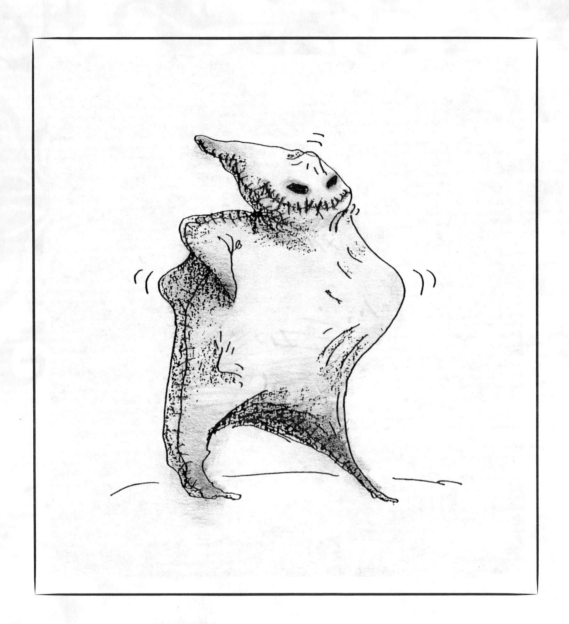

hear their screams, Oogie looked to see what had gone wrong. He found Jack sitting in their place.

"Jack! But they said you were dead!" Oogie edged away and stomped on a button that sent sword-wielding playing cards on Jack.

Jack escaped their slashing blades with skillful leaps.

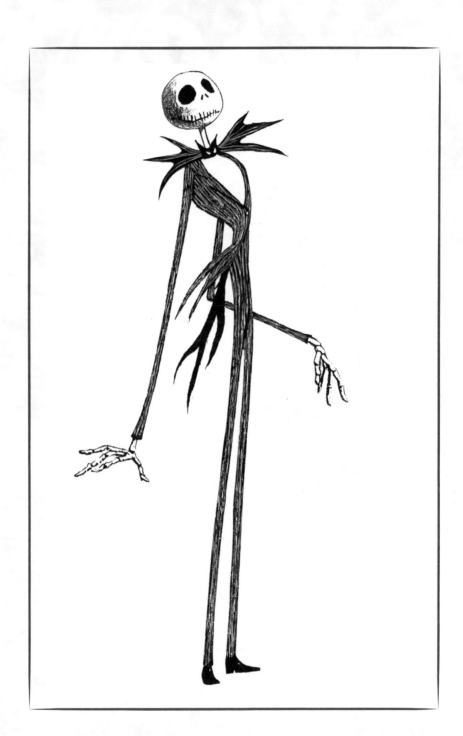

When Oogie saw that his attempts to destroy Jack weren't working, he hit yet another button, releasing a spinning saw from the roof.

Sally cried out to warn Jack of the blade swinging toward him. Jack leaped out of the way and landed face-to-face with Oogie.

But the monster had one more trick up his sleeve. Oogie cackled as he leaped onto a pendulum, which lifted him away, leaving Jack alone on the dangerous wheel.

But Oogie's plan was about to unravel . . . and so was he.

"How dare you treat my friends so shamefully!" Jack boomed, grasping a loose thread hanging from Oogie. As Oogie rose into the air, Jack pulled on the thread. The monster's seams unraveled, releasing the bugs inside.

"Now look what you've done!" Oogie cried, now a writhing mass of repulsive bugs. "My bugs!" he sobbed as his insects fell into the molten pit.

With Oogie defeated, Jack returned Santa's hat and apologized for making such a terrible mess of Christmas.

Santa told Jack that the next time he wanted to take over a holiday, he should listen to Sally.

"I hope there's still time," Jack said.

"To fix Christmas? Of course there is. I'm Santa Claus!" Santa replied, laying a finger on the side of his nose and flying into the chute.

SALLY'S DRESS

"He'll fix things, Jack. He knows what to do," Sally said.

"How did you get down here, Sally?" Jack asked, looking at Sally as if he were seeing her for the very first time.

"Oh, I was trying to . . . Well, I wanted to . . . to . . ." Sally tried to explain but was unable to meet his gaze.

"To help me?" Jack asked, placing a hand on her shoulder. "Sally, I can't believe I never realized that you—"

But he didn't get to finish. The Mayor, along with Lock, Shock, and Barrel, had arrived. They threw down a rope to rescue Jack and Sally.

Jack grasped Sally's hand, and they were pulled to safety.

***

In the normal world, Santa sped through the skies, stopping at every house to replace Jack's gruesome gifts with delightful presents made in Christmas Town.

"Good news, folks. Santa Claus, the one and only, has finally been spotted!" the news presenter announced.

In Halloween Town, people rejoiced to see the safe return of their pumpkin king. And Jack was happy too.

"It's great to be home!" Jack proclaimed.

"Happy Halloween!" Santa cried from his sleigh in the sky as he delivered a special gift to everyone in Halloween Town.

"Merry Christmas!" Jack called back as snowflakes filled the air.

Christmas had come to Halloween Town for the very first time.

Jack was happy that his friends finally understood the joy he had felt in Christmas Town. But Jack didn't join the fun. He still felt there was something missing, but this time Jack knew exactly what—or rather, who—it was.

Jack watched as Sally slipped through the graveyard gate. He followed her to the snow-covered graveyard and asked to join her on top of the hill. Together at last, Jack took Sally's rag doll hands in his and they kissed by the light of the full moon.

The End

———— ❧❧ ————

Tim Burton

Best known for directing Gothic and dark fantasy films, American director, producer, animator, writer, and artist Tim Burton began his career at Walt Disney Feature Animation, now known as the Walt Disney Animation Studios. Burton began making films at a young age and went on to study character animation at the California Institute of the Arts (CalArts). His student film *Stalk of the Celery Monster* earned him a place as an apprentice at Disney.

Burton's early career at Disney included animation work on films such as *The Fox and the Hound* and *The Black Cauldron*. In 1982, Burton created a stop-motion animation for the studio: a black-and-white short tribute to Vincent Price, titled *Vincent*. It was in the same year that Burton penned a poem he called "The Nightmare Before Christmas." The poem was on its way to becoming a 30-minute TV special or a short film, but development halted, and Burton left Disney in 1984. Over the years Burton thought about the project and, in 1990, returned to produce the poem as a full-length, stop-motion musical film in partnership with director Henry Selick.

Following the success of *The Nightmare Before Christmas*, Burton has gone on to collaborate with Disney on several projects, including the 1996 stop-motion movie *James and the Giant Peach*, which features a cameo from Jack Skellington; the 2010 film *Alice in Wonderland*; the 2016 sequel *Alice Through the Looking Glass*; and a 2019 live-action remake of Disney's *Dumbo*.

Concept art on pages 2-3, 8, 25, 35, 52, 65, 69, and 78-79.

The following pieces of concept art were likely done by Tim Burton: 17, 19, 23, 24, 31, 44, 45, 50, 55, 61, and 75.

———— ❧❧ ————

Kendal Cronkhite

Kendal Cronkhite began her film career working on *The Nightmare Before Christmas* as assistant art director. In 1996, she worked with fellow art director Bill Boes on *James and the Giant Peach*, taking on the role of art director. In 1998, Cronkhite moved to the newly founded DreamWorks Animation Studios to art direct the movie *Antz*. She has since worked as a production designer on other DreamWorks films, including the *Madagascar* series and, most recently, *Trolls* and *Trolls World Tour*.

Concept art on pages 7, 14, 22, 42, and 67.

The following pieces of concept art were possibly done by Kendal Cronkhite: 37, 50, and 73.

Miguel Domingo

Miguel Domingo, also known as Michael Cachuela, studied at CalArts under Joe Ranft for story and Chris Buck for animation. Domingo contributed to the 20th Century Fox film *FernGully: The Last Rainforest*, released in 1992, as a storyboard artist before working with Skellington Productions on *The Nightmare Before Christmas*. Domingo has since worked as a storyboard artist on Disney's *James and the Giant Peach* and Pixar's *The Incredibles* and *Ratatouille*.

Story sketches on pages 20 and 71.

Joe Ranft

Joe Ranft began studying in the character animation program at CalArts in 1978. His student film *Good Humor* was noticed by Disney executives, and he was offered a job at the studio. Ranft began his Disney career working on television projects, but his big break came when he moved to the Feature Animation department, working under Eric Larson. Ranft worked as a story artist, storyboard artist, and storyboard supervisor on many Disney and Pixar films, and even lent his voice to characters in *The Brave Little Toaster*, *Toy Story*, and *Cars*. For *The Nightmare Before Christmas*, Ranft took on the role of storyboard supervisor. Ranft tragically passed away in 2005, and his last film, *Cars,* was dedicated to his memory.

Story sketches on pages 26 and 27 (possibly), and 33.

Jørgen Klubien

Jørgen Klubien is an animation artist, writer, and singer. Klubien has worked as a character animator and storyboard artist on a number of Disney films, including *Oliver & Company*, *The Little Mermaid*, *The Rescuers Down Under*, *A Bug's Life*, and *Frankenweenie*. For *The Nightmare Before Christmas*, Klubien is credited with additional character design and also assisted with storyboards for the film. Klubien is also the lead singer of the Danish band Danseorkestret.

The following story sketches were possibly done by Jørgen Klubien: 26 and 27.

Deane Taylor

Deane Taylor is a layout artist, writer, art director, production supervisor, and director who has worked at Hanna-Barbera, Disney, and MGM Animation. For *The Nightmare Before Christmas*, Taylor served as art director, and he also appeared in the documentary short *The Making of Tim Burton's The Nightmare Before Christmas*.

The following concept art were possibly done by Deane Taylor: 37 and 73.

~⚬~

Kelly Asbury

American film director, screenwriter, story supervisor, voice actor, animator, children's book author and illustrator, and nonfiction author Kelly Asbury worked on many animated films in many different roles. Asbury graduated from CalArts, where he studied animation and filmmaking. He joined Disney to work on *The Black Cauldron* as an in-between artist, and went on to work on films including *The Little Mermaid*, *Beauty and the Beast*, *Gnomeo & Juliet*, and *Frozen*. Asbury worked as assistant art director on *The Nightmare Before Christmas*. Sadly, Asbury passed away in 2020 at the age of 60.

Concept art on pages 39, 48, and 77.

Bill Boes

California native Bill Boes is a production designer, art director, model maker, and special effects creator. Boes has worked across TV, live action, animation, and stop-motion animation. For *The Nightmare Before Christmas*, Boes took on the role of assistant art director and also worked as a model maker. Boes also contributed to Disney's 1996 stop-motion film *James and the Giant Peach*.

Concept art on page 57.

~⚬~

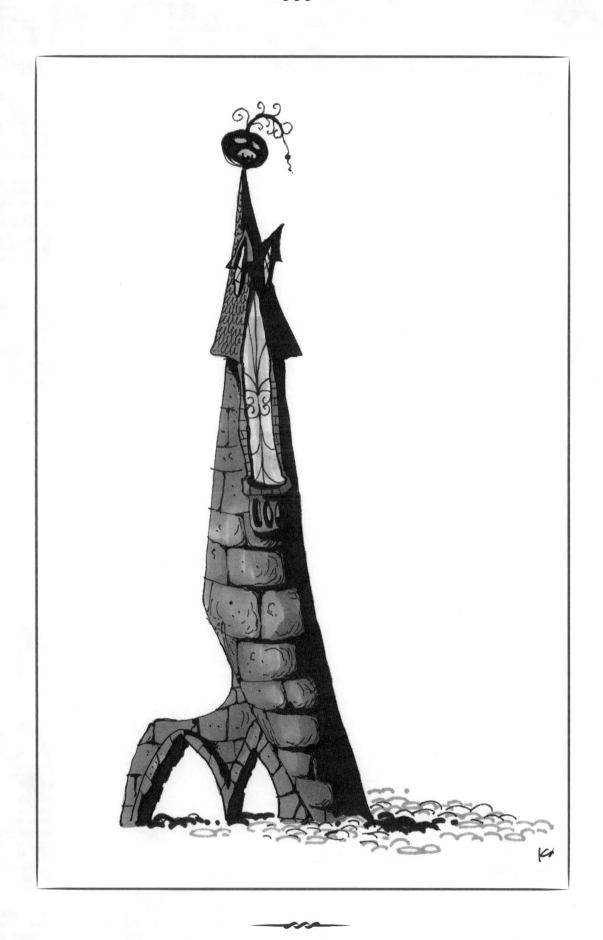

Glossary of Terms

Concept art: drawings, paintings, or sketches prepared in the early stages of a film's development. Concept art is often used to inspire the staging, mood, and atmosphere of scenes.

Production animation puppet: a character, often created from cloth or foam latex, fabricated around an articulated armature, that is manipulated by an animator in small increments and photographed one frame of film at a time in order to give it the illusion of movement.

Story sketch: shows the action that's happening in a scene, as well as presenting the emotion of the story moment. Story sketches help visualize the film before expensive resources are committed to its production.